The White Ballets

RAJKA KUPESIC

TUNDRA BOOKS

To the memory of a very special lady,
my beloved mama.

Text and illustrations copyright © 2011 by Rajka Kupesic

Published in Canada by Tundra Books,

75 Sherbourne Street, Toronto, Ontario M5A 2P9

Published in the United States by Tundra Books of Northern New York,

P.O. Box 1030, Plattsburgh, New York 12901

Library of Congress Control Number: 2011922894

Library and Archives Canada Cataloguing in Publication

Kupesic, Rajka

The white ballets / by Rajka Kupesic.

ISBN 978-0-88776-923-8

1. Ballets – Stories, plots, etc. – Juvenile literature. I. Title.

GV1790.A1K86 2011   J792.8'45   C2011-901229-4

We acknowledge the financial support of the Government of Canada through the Book Publishing

Industry Development Program (BPIDP) and that of the Government of Ontario through the

Ontario Media Development Corporation's Ontario Book Initiative. We further acknowledge the support

of the Canada Council for the Arts and the Ontario Arts Council for our publishing program.

The paintings for this book were rendered in oils and gold leaf

Design: Jennifer Lum

Printed and bound in China

1 2 3 4 5 6   16 15 14 13 12 11

~Ballet Blanc~

THE TRIUMPH OF THE CORPS DE BALLET

When I imagined making this book, my first thought was of the *ballets blancs* or white ballets. *"Ballet blanc"* refers to the identical white costumes worn by the group of female dancers in the *corps de ballet*.

The *corps* is much more than a decorative backdrop for the prima ballerina. It is a character unto itself, and its power lies in uniformity rather than individuality. *Corps* choreography creates striking patterns that, when repeated, have a hypnotic affect on the audience.

A *corps* member must master the art of moving as one with her peers, performing the same steps with the same height of leg, the same angle of head, and the same facial expression. This requires endless hours of practice.

I chose *Swan Lake* and *Giselle* because they were among the first ballets I performed as a young ballerina and later, as a graduate of the National Ballet School in Zagreb. *La Bayadère* was long-hidden behind the "iron curtain" in the former USSR. As a result, I never had the chance to dance in it. I learned about *La Bayadère* much later, and have loved it ever since. All three ballets are among the most significant works in the Romantic *ballet blanc* style.

I dedicated this book to my mother, whose dream it was to see me become a ballerina. I wanted to pay homage to her through another form of artistic expression. My paintings are not meant to be literal depictions of the stories they accompany. Instead, they are meant to portray the essence of a performance; to give a sense of staging and costume, symbolism and meaning, artistry and music. In short, they are meant to pass the magic of the white ballets on to you.

Swan Lake

Everyone, rich and poor, was invited to the palace garden to celebrate Prince Siegfried's birthday. They came gladly, for he was a favorite with them all. What feasting and drinking! What dancing and singing – until the joyous music stopped.

The queen, not one to feast or dance or sing, swept into the garden and summoned the prince to her side. Siegfried braced himself for a lecture.

"Another year has passed, my son, and you are a grown man. It is time to put childish things behind you."

Siegfried had heard this many times and was about to go back to his friends, but the queen clutched his arm. "You will be king one day, and you will need a wife by your side. I have arranged a royal ball tomorrow night and have invited several beautiful princesses. You are to choose one to marry."

The prince sighed. It was true. Soon he would be king, and a king needed a queen.

"I have something for you." The queen signaled for an attendant to bring the gift. She took it and laid it in Siegfried's arms.

Siegfried was thrilled. It was a sleek, new bow fashioned from rare and costly wood. "It is perfect, Mother. I –" Before he could finish, the queen turned and left.

As the musicians took up their instruments once more, the sound of beating wings filled the air. Everyone looked up to see wild swans soaring above. "Let's go after them!" cried Siegfried's friends. Quickly, they formed a hunting party.

But the prince suddenly felt like being alone. He let the others go on ahead. Soon he came to a lake, set in a clearing like a dark jewel among the rocks. A castle towered above it from a high cliff.

Prince Siegfried was astonished by what happened next. As the castle clock struck twelve, a snow-white swan wearing a golden crown landed on the lake and transformed into the loveliest maiden he had ever seen. The prince stepped forward, but she trembled with fright.

"I won't hurt you," he said, placing his bow on the ground. "Tell me your name."

"I am Odette, the Swan Queen. I was once a human princess, but the magician, Rothbart, cast a terrible spell on me. Now I am doomed to be a swan from sun up to midnight. My poor mother's tears have formed this lake."

Outraged, the prince blurted out a vow. "Odette, I promise to break the spell." As soon as he said the words, he knew that he had won her heart. The prince had many questions to ask, but someone was calling to Odette.

"I must go," she cried. "How I wish I could stay!"

Just then, a group of terrified maidens in white feather dresses burst into the clearing, followed by Siegfried's friends. The hunters did not know they were about to shoot at innocent girls cursed by evil magic.

The Swan Queen stood before them. "I implore you not to kill us," she cried.

"Lower your weapons!" ordered the prince. Baffled, his friends did as he said.

"Thank you," said Odette with grateful tears in her eyes.

"I cannot bear this," Seigfried said. "How can I free you from this dreadful curse?"

"Only by pledging your eternal love, but if you break your vow, I will remain a swan forever."

Thunder crashed, as a great cloud darkened the sky. Rothbart appeared, laughing wildly. Siegfried reached for his bow, but Odette stopped him.

"If Rothbart dies, the spell will never be broken." With that, her human form changed, and she became a swan again.

Prince Siegfried and his friends looked back in wonder as they left the forest.

❧

Garlands of flowers perfumed the air and the glow of candlelight danced on the stone walls of the palace. It was the evening of the queen's ball. The guests were dressed in their richest silks and satins. As promised, the queen had invited several princesses to meet her son. Though he danced with them all, Siegfried knew that his heart belonged to Odette.

"Have you made your choice?" asked his mother.

Before the prince could say anything, Rothbart the magician swept into the hall. With him was a ravishing maiden dressed in gleaming black. Siegfried thought he recognized the Swan Queen.

"Mother, this is the one who will be my bride!" he announced joyfully.

Rothbart's face twisted into a monstrous grin. "Are you sure, Siegfried? Will you pledge your eternal love to her?"

The young man was so happy to see his Swan Queen that he didn't notice the ice-cold, wicked eyes of the maiden before him. "I pledge – "

No sooner had he uttered the words than a bolt of lightning flashed and sizzled around Rothbart and the maiden.

"You fool! I would never give you Odette!" Rothbart snarled. "Meet your new bride – my daughter, Odile." Rothbart laughed insanely.

Outside at the window, Odette watched the terrible scene unfold until she could bear it no longer. Blinded by tears, she fled into the forest.

At last, Prince Siegfried looked more closely at Odile. Sure enough, this was not the girl he loved. He had to find Odette. Perhaps she was at the lake where he'd first met her. He bade his mother good-bye and rushed away from the palace, Rothbart's cry ringing in his ears. "Search as much as you like, but you will never have Odette!"

A storm raged as Siegfried raced to the lake. Rothbart had flown to it before the prince. He stood high on the cliff in front of his castle. The swan maidens clung together by the shore, the wild wind and rain whipping their feather dresses.

Frantic, Prince Siegfried ran from one to another. "Where is Odette? What's happened to Odette?" he cried. And suddenly – finally – she was in his arms.

"I cannot live any longer under this evil curse. My dear mother's tears made this lake, and now it shall be my grave," she said.

"Nor can I live without you. I will follow you, even to your grave." The lovers held hands, and together they stepped toward the water. As they did, a mighty flash of lightning engulfed Rothbart.

"I am destroyed! Your love has conquered me!" he shrieked. His castle crumbled to the earth as the mad magician vanished, never to be seen again.

With the first rays of the rising sun, the curse was broken. Odette was no longer the Swan Queen, but she became Prince Siegfried's bride, and the royal couple lived long and happily ever after.

ABOUT *Swan Lake*

This story crosses sorcery and mystical creatures with the real world, where betrayal and power are ultimately conquered by love and loyalty. Premiering in Moscow, *Swan Lake* was not a big success initially. It was the first ballet set to the score of a symphonic composer, and people didn't accept it easily. Before Tchaikovsky, ballet scores were usually written by "specialists" who preferred decorative melodies and light rhythms. When Tchaikovsky died in 1893, a renewal of the ballet, including a new second act choreographed by Les Ivanov, was staged. The performance was a great success and led to the 1895 premiere of the version we know today. Only then did Tchaikovsky's score gain recognition. Now he is known as the most important ballet composer of all.

For the *corps de ballet*, *Swan Lake* is difficult. It is also a unique challenge for the prima ballerina, who must dance two opposite characters: Odette, the gentle white swan, and Odile, the evil black swan. I first performed in *Swan Lake* as a *corps* member when I was only fourteen and still in ballet school. That first and very challenging role had a huge impact on me. To this day, I vividly remember the entire sequence of steps I had to perfect. I also remember pointing my feet while running in circles with my fellow swans, making identical foot movements in unison with the bird ahead of me and forcing my arms as far behind my shoulders as possible to create the illusion of wings.

The first painting focuses on the captivating beauty and majesty of swans. Creatures such as sylphs, Wilis, Shades, water nymphs, and swans enjoyed great popularity when the *ballets blancs* were created. In *Swan Lake* the forces of good and evil are so closely linked, it is almost impossible to separate them, as the unfortunate Prince Siegfried discovers. I have framed my swans with gold and set them against a rising curtain: the magic begins. The four corner birds are beaded with water droplets, or are those the tears of a mother's longing for her lost child? The sinister castle below overshadows the lake, almost blocking the rising moon's glow. Veiled in mist, the swans are transforming into beautiful maidens.

The next painting is the classic *ballet blanc* scene. Prince Siegfried carries the crossbow his mother has given him for his birthday. Alone in the forest, he spots the Swan Queen, Odette, among the beautiful swan maidens and falls in love with her. They dance in the leafy glade for the few precious hours she can assume her human form. At the bottom, a pair of swans reminds us that at dawn, the maidens will disappear. This scene is deceptively peaceful. Look in the upper part of the painting, and you may find where I have hidden the evil sorcerer, Rothbart, who has Odette under his spell. In the form of an owl, he watches everything below.

Painting three, known in ballet as the grand scene, fills the stage. In Classical ballets, there is often a set of character dances that lend beauty to these scenes. Here, exotic princesses hope to win Prince Siegfried's affection. But they will wait a long time, for Odile, daughter of Rothbart, has arrived dressed as the black swan. Siegfried is enchanted by her, and believing that she is Odette, declares his eternal love. At the castle window, Odette hears Siegfried's apparent betrayal, and the final drama begins. I have put my white swan in that window and composed the painting so that the eye is drawn to her, even though she is so tiny. I am very proud of her lighting!

At the bottom of the fourth painting, Rothbart, in the form of the evil owl, is crushed by eternal love. At the top, young maidens who were once swans are now free. The prince and Odette sail to their future in a regal swan ship, no longer in shadow, but under a dazzling sun. It took me over a month to apply the "dazzle" with slivers of gold leaf! The teardrops from painting one have been replaced with precious stones, and the future king and queen are together.

Giselle

In a country cottage, there lived a lovely peasant girl named Giselle. More than anything, Giselle loved to dance, but her mother worried constantly. "My girl," she'd warn, "please be careful. Your heart . . . Too much dancing could . . ." But to Giselle, dancing was far more important than a weak heart.

And now she had much to dance about. She was in love with a handsome newcomer to the village who went by the name of Loys. Loys would often hide among the trees and watch as Giselle danced for the joy of it. Soon, he too, was in love.

Poor, trusting Giselle couldn't know that Loys was not at all who he seemed. He was no peasant, and his name was not Loys. It was Count Albrecht. Worse, he was engaged to a highborn lady, far better suited to be a count's bride than a peasant girl.

One autumn morning, Giselle danced close to Albrecht as he watched. He caught her arm, startling her a little. "Rest awhile with me," he said. He led her to a bench and they sat while she playfully picked a flower.

"He loves me, he loves me not," she counted, plucking each petal. The last one was unlucky. "He loves me not!"

"You must have counted wrong, Giselle, I couldn't love you more." He held out his hand, and they danced to the beating of their hearts, until breathless, they stopped to kiss.

Now, a village boy named Hilarion had been watching them. He'd loved Giselle since they were children. When he saw the kiss, he cried out.

Giselle tried to calm him. "We've done nothing wrong, Hilarion. We were only dancing." But Hilarion was jealous and grew angrier. He shoved Albrecht hard.

Just as the two were about to come to blows, the happy townsfolk appeared, celebrating a good harvest. Although she was already tired and should have known better, Giselle couldn't resist. She joined their festival as they danced to the village. Partway there, she swooned and would have fallen to the ground, had Albrecht not been there to catch her.

Someone fetched Giselle's mother, who came and took her home. The others returned to the celebration – all except Hilarion. He was suspicious of the stranger. "Who is this fellow? Perhaps I'll find a clue in his cottage," he muttered.

Not long after, a hunting party of lords and ladies stopped at Giselle's home. A nobleman asked her mother if she could give them food and drink, and he gave her a gold coin for her trouble. Giselle and her mother brought cheese and bread, cakes and wine.

The guests ate their fill. One lady was especially beautiful. Giselle didn't know that she was Bathilde, Albrecht's intended. Bathilde wore a gorgeous gown, and Giselle couldn't help touching it. Realizing that Bathilde had seen her, she blushed, ashamed.

Bathilde was as kind as she was lovely. "What is your name, my dear?"

"I am Giselle, my lady."

"And how do you pass your time, Giselle?"

"Well, I sew and I weave, but most of all, I love to dance."

"Is there someone special you dance for?" Bathilde's voice sounded like a silver bell.

Giselle blushed again. "Yes, and I will marry him soon."

The answer delighted Bathilde. "I, too, am soon to wed! Would you kindly dance for me?"

Giselle had already danced more than should have that day, but she could not refuse the lady. She danced sweetly while the nobles clapped and her mother worried. Relieved when the dance ended, Giselle's mother led everyone into the cottage to rest.

But there was to be no rest. The harvesters returned, their arms heavy with bunches of grapes. "Giselle, Giselle, come out," called Albrecht at the cottage door. "I have something for you." When she appeared, Albrecht held out a wreath. "We've all decided. You are to be the Queen of the Harvest." He took her hand. "Come, dance for us, my queen!"

"You've had quite enough dancing for one day, Giselle," interrupted her mother. "I forbid you to take one more step!" But everyone begged until she gave in. "If you must dance, then dance. But be careful. Oh, please be careful, Giselle."

The others clapped as Giselle twirled faster and faster. Suddenly, Hilarion appeared, his face like a thunder cloud. In his hands he held a hunting horn and an ornate sword.

"This man is not who he seems! What peasant has a horn like this, or a sword like this?" He flourished them at the surprised villagers. Albrecht lunged for the sword. Before he could grab it, Hilarion blew the horn as loudly as he could.

The sound brought the hunting party out of the cottage. Bathilde smiled when she saw her beloved. "Why, Albrecht! What are you doing here? And why are you dressed like that?"

Albrecht was speechless, but Giselle was not. "Albrecht? No. His name is Loys!"

Bathilde laughed. "You must be mistaken, my dear. This is Count Albrecht, the man I am to marry."

"But that's impossible. He says he loves . . . " Giselle stopped. A terrible chill came over her. Slowly, she began to dance in a delirious, frenzied state.

The others watched in dismay. Their dismay soon turned to horror. Giselle was staring at something only she could see. "Aren't they lovely, Mother? See how their white dresses float in the air?"

"Giselle, my child, no!" cried her poor mother. Before she could reach her daughter, Giselle crumpled to the ground. And there she died of a broken heart.

Hilarion was devastated. He visited Giselle's grave in the forest and marked the spot with a wooden cross. He lingered until the light began to fade, though he knew that the forest was a dangerous place for a young man, come nightfall. He had heard what happened to maidens who died before their wedding day. In their sorrow they became restless spirits called Wilis. Dressed in ghostly bridal white, the Wilis roamed the night woods. If they came upon a young man, they forced him to dance and dance until he died of exhaustion.

Hilarion was about to leave when a quick movement caught his eye. He whispered a hasty prayer and fled toward home. He was right to do so, for he had seen a Wili. One by one, spirit maidens dressed in white, like the brides they would never be, emerged from the darkness and began their ghostly dance of death. As they swooped and turned, Giselle stirred and rose from her grave to join them, for she too, had become a Wili.

And now it was Albrecht, blinded by tears, who stumbled to Giselle's grave. "If only I could hold you again, my love!" he sobbed. Then, sensing that he was not alone, he looked up. Giselle stood before him, just beyond his grasp. She showered him with fragrant white lilies, then entered his embrace.

The other Wilis had no thoughts of love, for they had captured Hilarion on his way out of the forest. He begged them for mercy, but they forced him into their eternal dance until he could barely lift his feet. In the end, he was lost: the Wilis danced him to death. And then they turned to Albrecht.

Giselle pleaded with Myrtha, Queen of the Wilis to spare his life, but she would not listen. Desperate, Giselle drew Albrecht to the wooden cross that Hilarion had placed on her grave. The Wilis fell back, for this was a power much stronger than theirs. They could not capture Albrecht unless they enticed him to leave the protection of the cross. So they did a wicked thing; they invited the lovers to dance.

The chance to dance together again was too powerful for Giselle and Albrecht to resist. They leapt and turned and soared. Albrecht swooned, but as weary as he was, he could not stop. The Wilis' voices filled the forest: "Dance, Albrecht! Dance our dance of death."

Giselle knew that their spell would be broken with the coming of dawn. This time it was she who whispered, "Dance, Albrecht, dance." If only she could keep him on his feet until first light, he would be saved.

Albrecht could barely take another step or lift his heavy arms, but Giselle would not let him stop. Out of love for her he tried, until at last he fell to the ground, exhausted. But as he did, the sweet chime of morning bells rang out. Albrecht had been saved.

The Wilis faded into the morning mist. Myrtha beckoned Giselle to follow. For one last time, she held her beloved Albrecht in her arms. But the sun reached her, and she too, vanished, never to return.

❦ ABOUT *Giselle* ❧

Giselle is a two-act ballet that premiered at the Paris Opera in 1841 and included all the ingredients of Romantic works: a magical creature, a mysterious setting, star-crossed lovers, and of course, the *corps de ballet*. But *Giselle* had something different. It marked the beginning of the era of ballerinas dancing *en pointe*. The dancer *en pointe* represented the perfect woman, the lighter-than-air figure who was a figment of imagined beauty. For the first time, toe dancing was elevated from a series of tricks to an art form.

The music for this landmark ballet was composed by Adolphe Charles Adam, whose work was admired by Tchaikovsky. He used a technique called *leitmotif*, with recurring themes for certain characters. Tchaikovsky later borrowed this technique for his *Swan Lake* and *Sleeping Beauty*. Marius Petipa revived *Giselle* in 1903 and put the finishing touches to it just in time for the rising Russian star, Anna Pavlova, to dance the starring role.

It was Petipa who introduced and perfected the second-act *ballet blanc*, which has become a symbol of Classical ballet. Again, I have powerful memories of that second act, when, as a Wili, I made the long, grueling journey across the stage and back with one leg lifted behind and the other slightly bent (in *plié*). My Wili companions and I slid in small, rhythmical movements, passing each other on our *arabesque voyage*. Look for us in the upper section of the last image.

The first painting shows Giselle's young friends dancing to celebrate the grape harvest. In the middle, we see the famous "he loves me, he loves me not" scene where Giselle's affection for the handsome newcomer blossoms like a flower. This scene features a musical *leitmotif*, which we hear throughout the first act whenever Giselle appears. At the bottom of the painting, Giselle dances with Prince Albrecht, who claims to be Loys, a stranger to the village. I have layered this apparently happy scene with a sense of foreboding. Giselle's concerned mother is in the front bottom left, fretting about her daughter's fragile health. In the middle ground, Hilarion, a village boy who loves Giselle, watches with envy from behind a tree. In sharp contrast to Giselle's humble cottage, Albrecht's castle home dominates the background, almost announcing Albrecht's deception and his promise to live there with his intended bride, Bathilde. The three threats to Giselle's happiness are all present: her poor health, a jealous rival, and the status she can never attain.

In the second painting, the "mad scene," Giselle realizes that Albrecht has betrayed her. In shock and sorrow, she looks back on the history of their romance. The flower in her hands reminds us of the petal-counting that ended with "he loves me not." Thinking back on events leading up to this betrayal, Giselle enters a state of madness. I have painted her hair, loose and entangled with everything that has contributed to her undoing. Her pale skin and vacant eyes are signs that her heart is truly breaking. At the bottom, Giselle lies dead, as Albrecht holds her in his arms. Giselle's pain is over. With the realization of what he has done, Albrecht's is just beginning. I have framed both vignettes with Easter lilies, symbols of resurrection, purity, and hope. You will find them again in the next painting.

In the third painting Giselle has become a Wili – the restless soul of a maiden who has been betrayed by love and has died before her wedding day. The souls of other girls welcome her, and two of them place a crown of lilies in her hair. It replaces the harvest crown Giselle recently wore, and the one she will never have as Albrecht's bride. In her arms, I have placed a bouquet of trumpet-shaped white lilies. Are they from Albrecht? Hilarion? No, they are my tribute to one of the best-loved title characters of all time.

The narrow band at the top of the fourth painting is the scene where the Wilis perform their *ballet blanc* dance. Below them, the mystic woods conceal Giselle's last act of love. Even in death, she has managed to keep the exhausted Albrecht alive. As Myrtha, Queen of the Willis, beckons her away, she passes her flowers on to the prince in a final act of forgiveness. They will be with him when he awakes at dawn.

La Bayadère

Nikiya had always longed to be a *bayadère*. Temple dancers, were the luckiest girls in the land. They walked in cool gardens on rose-scented paths and wore silks and had rings of tinkling silver bells at their fingertips. All they had to do was dance for the temple priests and the gods! Nikiya could imagine no better life.

One day, the temple priest, or High Brahmin, passed by her father's hut and asked the girl to bring him water. She fetched it and handed him the dipper.

"What is your name, child?" the High Brahmin asked.

"Nikiya," she answered shyly, staring at her toes.

"Such grace! Such a sweet smile! You must come to the temple and learn to dance." With those few words Nikiya's dream came true. But that was only the beginning of her story.

Nikiya worked hard to prove worthy of being a *bayadère*. She learned so quickly that even the ruler, Rajah Dugmanta, noticed her. Before long she was given a great honor.

A courtier sought her out during a practice with the other girls. "Nikiya! I have exciting news. The Rajah wants you to dance this evening to welcome his victorious warriors home from battle!"

She was nervous, but that evening she danced more beautifully than she ever had. The bravest of the warriors, Solor, was spellbound.

After everyone had retired, Solor found Nikiya in the garden.

He was almost as shy as she, for though he tried to be witty and clever, all he could think to say was "What's your name? Mine is Solor." But soon the words began to flow between them. By dawn, the two had pledged their love to each other.

As it happened, Solor was not free to make such a pledge. The next morning there was an announcement from the palace. The Rajah had picked Solor to marry his daughter Gamzatti. And who would dance at their wedding but Nikiya!

The temple always buzzed with gossip, and soon the High Brahmin learned that Solor and Nikiya were lovers. Poor Nikiya did not suspect that the High Brahmin had wanted her for himself ever since she'd handed him that dipper of water in front of her home. The High Brahmin seethed with envy. He must get rid of Solor!

He hurried to the palace with a devious plan. He asked for an audience with the Rajah, and was led into the presence of the ruler. "Rajah Dugmanta, I am sorry to bear troubling news. You have chosen Solor to marry the princess. Perhaps you are unaware that he has pledged his love to the *bayadère*, Nikiya. Surely you will have him put to death for his treachery!"

The High Brahmin waited, trying not to look pleased with himself. But when the Rajah spoke, the words dismayed him.

"If what you say is true, then it is Nikiya who must die."

Now, Gamzatti had been eavesdropping and heard her father. She sent for Nikiya.

"This is a pouch full of rubies and sapphires, *Bayadère*. If you know what is good for you, forsake Solor, and it will be yours." She ran her fingers through the gleaming gems.

Nikiya was outraged. "I would never do such a thing! My love has no price!"

As arguments often do, this one made both girls forget their senses. Before Nikiya knew it, she had grabbed a dagger, and in a fit of rage lunged at the princess.

Gamzatti's maid, rushed into the room. "Whatever are you doing? Stop this immediately!"

Nikiya dropped the dagger as if it were a burning ember. "I'm so sorry, I don't know what came over me," she cried. "Please forgive me." Horrified at what she had almost done, she fled. But Gamzatti could be as cold and cruel as her father. She did not accept the apology. Like the Rajah before her, she decided that Nikiya must die.

Though her heart was heavy, on the day of the engagement celebration Nikiya performed as she had been ordered to do. She danced as beautifully as ever, and when she was finished, one of the temple dancers placed a basket of flowers in her arms.

These must be from Solor, she thought, breathing in their spicy perfume. But the basket was not from her beloved. It was from Rajah Dugmanta and Princess Gamzatti, and hidden within their gift was a poisonous snake.

Again, Nikiya buried her face in the blooms, and the deadly serpent darted out, striking her on the neck.

The High Brahmin tried to help, for he truly loved the *bayadère*. "Quick, Nikiya – drink this. It will save you!" he cried. He held out a vial of potion to act against the venom.

Nikiya pushed it away. "I don't wish to live without Solor." These words were the last she ever spoke before falling to the ground, dead.

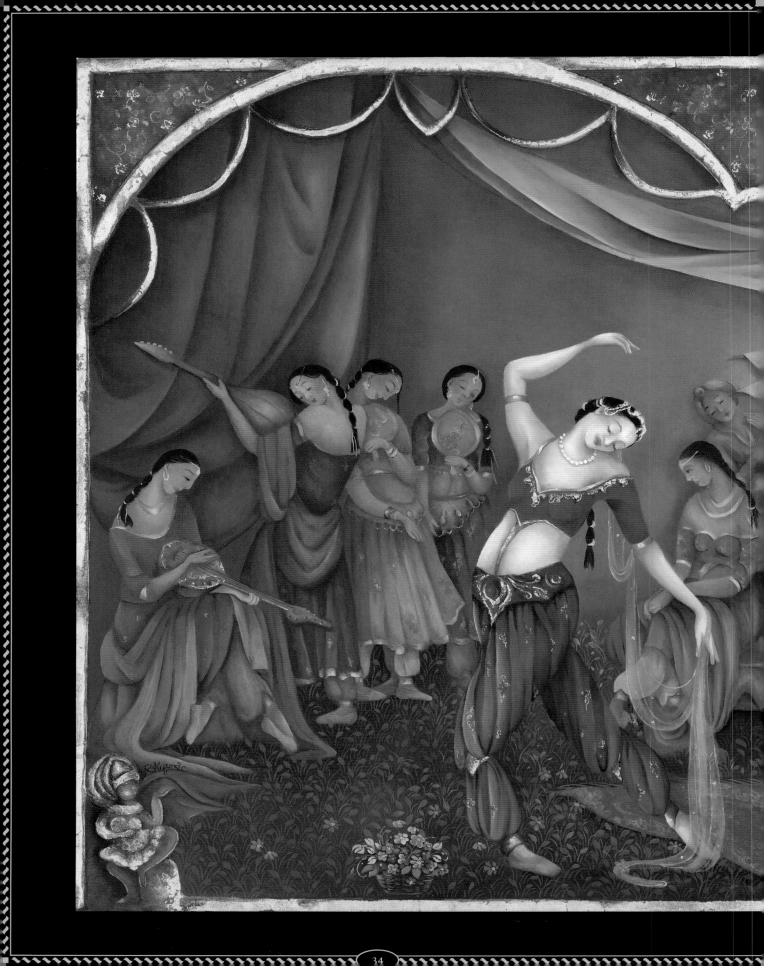

When Solor saw that Nikiya was truly gone, he retreated to his darkened room where he wept until he had no more tears. He could not eat or drink or speak.

The only comfort Solor found came from smoking his water pipe. Finally – mercifully – he fell asleep. In his drug-induced dream he saw Nikiya's Shade, her spirit, dancing in a land he knew to be the Kingdom of the Shades. He'd heard of this place, far away at the top of a high, high mountain. Solor's spirit joined hers, and together with the ghosts of other *bayadères* they danced as they had never danced before. They danced until Solor's heart was soothed.

But dreams die with the morning light. When Solor awoke, he heard the sounds of wedding preparations for his marriage to Gamzatti.

With clumsy fingers, Solor dressed. Slowly he made his way to the temple where the wedding was to take place. He took no notice of the ornate marble building or of the High Brahmin or of his beautiful bride, Gamzatti. His thoughts were filled with Nikiya, or rather with the memory of her. It was her spirit that he loved, not with the flesh-and-blood princess who stood before him.

Solor was hardly aware that the time had come for the High Brahmin to seal the marriage by joining the hands of the bride and groom. The moment Solor's hand touched Gamzatti's, a rumble louder and more terrible than anyone had ever heard before, shook the ground. The temple and all within it were destroyed.

At last, Nikiya's and Solor's souls were free to belong to each other. Legend has it that they dwell at the top of the highest mountain in the world. If you visit it, there among the snow-covered peaks, perhaps you will see them dancing joyfully in the never-ending wind.

ABOUT *La Bayadère*

As with *Swan Lake* and *Giselle*, *La Bayadère* was choreographed by Marius Petipa.

The most celebrated and enduring passage of *La Bayadère* was the grand scene known as "The Kingdom of the Shades." Petipa's choreography for the entrance of the *corps de ballet* was to become one of his most celebrated compositions. In the last painting I have placed the *corps* dancing this segment in honor of his mastery.

Czech composer Ludwig Minkus worked with Petipa, to create some of the most celebrated ballets in the Classical style. He was a "specialist" composer, and he had the ability to evoke emotions with his scores, without being overpowering.

Although *La Bayadère* predates *Swan Lake* and was a classic in Russia, the work was almost completely unknown to the West, until the Kirov Ballet performed "The Kingdom of the Shades" in Paris in July of 1961, the same year Rudolf Nureyev defected.

Two years later, Nureyev staged and starred in the first full performance of *La Bayadère* outside of Russia, with Margot Fonteyn as Nikiya. The pairing was magnificent. The premiere was a resounding success and is considered to be among the most important moments in the history of ballet.

The first painting introduces the ballet, set in Royal India. The word *bayadère* comes from the Portuguese word *ballar*, which means "dancer." Here, you meet the temple dancer, Nikiya, along with her friends. In India, temple dancers held an important place in society. At the four corners, I have painted Shiva, the god and master of dance. Ancient

Hindus believed that dance was created by nature. The appearance of constellations, the movement of rivers, the waves in the seas, and the fluttering of leaves produced images of dancing in their minds. To them, dance represented the movements of the universe.

The next painting introduces all of the characters important to the plot. In the middle are Nikiya and Solor in love's embrace. At bottom right is Gamzatti, a wealthy Rajah's daughter, hopelessly in love with Solor. On the left is the High Brahmin who loves Nikiya. Note how the right feet of Nikya and Solor are planted solidly together, while their left feet point directly to the people that fate seems to have in store for them. The golden idol in the middle is in a neutral pose, favoring no one, yet almost questioning the fates with his raised arms.

In the grand scene, we are at the engagement of Solor and Gamzatti. I have tried to portray the elegance and opulence of the Rajah's palace. Costuming in this scene lends to the importance of this traditional betrothal ceremony. Solor and Nikiya are trying their best to comply with what they must face, but there is no love in Solor's stance, nor is there joy in Nikiya's last dance on earth.

The final scene represents the beautiful *ballet blanc* and Petipa's masterpiece. Solor, grieving Nikiya's death and under the influence of opium, dreams of being reunited with her in The Kingdom of Shades. In the Kirov Ballet version, this is the final act, for in the former USSR, it was felt that gods destroying a temple was not appropriate. Western versions often have a third act in which Solor wakes from his dream, realizes that he must marry Gamzatti, but goes mad, knowing she murdered Nikiya. The temple crumbles, and his spirit joins Nikiya's in eternity.

I have framed the dream with two golden peacocks. They are India's national birds and are symbols of renewal and longevity. Ancient belief has it that they guarded the gates to paradise. In India, the peacock was said to be the slayer of serpents and therefore a protector. This pair is here to protect and comfort Nikiya and Solor.

In the sky I have tried to evoke the magical entrance of the Shades. As they descend from above in endless *arabesque penchée* movements, there is a suggestion of their spiritual home at the top of Mount Everest.

One Last Word

Now that you know a little more about *ballets blancs*, go back and find the moon. She floats above each story. I say *she* because the moon is a symbol of femininity, purity, wisdom, and forgiveness. Sometimes she is referred to as the triple moon: the maiden, the mother, and the crone. The moon reflects light, and in so doing, reflects our worst fears and grandest hopes. A night with no moon is dark, indeed. A full moon lights our way and offers peace. It is no accident that I have added her magical presence to the darkest hour of each of these white ballets.